The Tourist at the End of the Universe

The Tourist at the End of the Universe

From Italian *Topolino* #1353, 1981
Writer: Carlo Chendi
Artist: Giorgio Cavazzano
Colorists: Digikore Studios with Travis and Nicole Seitler
Letterers: Nicole and Travis Seitler
Translation and Dialogue: Jonathan Gray

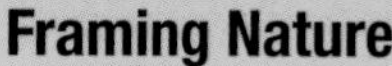

Framing Nature

From Czech *Kacer Donald* #12/2011
Writer & Artist: Daan Jippes
Colorists: Egmont with Travis and Nicole Seitler
Letterers: Nicole and Travis Seitler with Daan Jippes
Dialogue: Byron Erickson

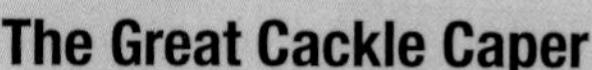

The Great Cackle Caper

From Italian *Almanacco Topolino* #234, 1976
Artist: Marco Rota
Colorists: Disney Italia and Digikore Studios
Letterers: Nicole and Travis Seitler
Translation and Dialogue: Jonathan Gray

The Terrible Thinking-Cap Tussle

From Danish *Anders And & Co.* #46/1965
Writer: Vic Lockman
Artist: Tony Strobl
Inker: Steve Steere
Colorist: Digikore Studios
Letterers: Nicole and Travis Seitler
Dialogue: Vic Lockman and Joe Torcivia

Waste Makes Haste

From Swedish *Kalle Anka & Co.* #47/2014
Writer: Lars Jensen
Artist: Daniel Pérez
Colorist: Digikore Studios
Letterers: Nicole and Travis Seitler
Dialogue: Joe Torcivia

Special thanks to Eugene Paraszczuk, Julie Dorris, Carlotta Quattrocolo, Manny Mederos, Chris Troise, Roberto Santillo, Camilla Vedove, and Stefano Ambrosio. | For international rights, contact licensing@idwpublishing.com

ISBN: 978-1-68405-317-9

21 20 19 18 1 2 3 4

IDW®
www.IDWPUBLISHING.com

Greg Goldstein, President & Publisher • Robbie Robbins, EVP & Sr. Art Director • Matthew Ruzicka, CPA, Chief Financial Officer
David Hedgecock, Associate Publisher • Lorelei Bunjes, VP of Digital Services • Eric Moss, Sr. Director, Licensing & Business Development

Ted Adams, Founder & CEO of IDW Media Holdings

Facebook: facebook.com/idwpublishing • Twitter: @idwpublishing • YouTube: youtube.com/idwpublishing
Tumblr: tumblr.idwpublishing.com • Instagram: instagram.com/idwpublishing

Originally published as UNCLE SCROOGE #29–31 (Legacy #433–435).

Sins of the Sorcery Summit

From Dutch *Donald Duck* #44/2014
Writer: Jan Kruse
Artist: Sander Gulien
Colorists: Sanoma with Travis and Nicole Seitler and David Gerstein
Letterers: Nicole and Travis Seitler
Translation and Dialogue: Jonathan Gray

Halloween Shivers

From Italian *Topolino* #2183, 1997
Writer: Nino Russo
Artist: Alessandro Barbucci
Colorists: Disney Italia and Digikore Studios
Letterers: Nicole and Travis Seitler
Translation and Dialogue: David Gerstein

Belle, Book and Bungle

From Danish *Anders And & Co.* #9/2014
Writer: Lars Jensen
Artist: Noel Van Horn
Colorist: Digikore Studios
Letterers: Nicole and Travis Seitler
Translation and Dialogue: Joe Torcivia and Lars Jensen

Celebrity Crushed

From Italian *Topolino* #3045, 2014
Writer: Vito Stabile
Artist: Enrico Faccini
Colorists: Disney Italia with Nicole and Travis Seitler
Letterers: Nicole and Travis Seitler
Translation and Dialogue: Thad Komorowski

Series Editor: Chris Cerasi
Archival Editor: David Gerstein

Cover Artist: Marco Mazzarello
Cover Colorist: Mario Perotta
Collection Editors: Justin Eisinger and Alonzo Simon
Collection Designer: Clyde Grapa
Publisher: Greg Goldstein

WALT DISNEY'S

UNCLE $CROOGE

and

THE TOURIST AT THE END OF THE UNIVERSE

CRAZY CHARACTERS TUMBLE IN AND OUT OF **SCROOGE McDUCK'S** DAILY LIFE! BUT ONE CHARACTER IS ABOUT TO MAKE A PARTICULARLY **LONG-LASTING** IMPRESSION ON HIM...

Originally published in *Topolino* #1353 (Italy, 1981)

ER... YOU OKAY, MR. McDUCK? YOU LOOK KINDA SICK!
YEUGH! YEAH... I'M JUST A LITTLE DIZZY, IS ALL!
RUMBLE!

HM... MAYBE YOU SHOULD SEE A DOCTOR!
NO, NO... I KNOW WHAT IT IS...

I HAVEN'T EATEN IN TWO DAYS! AHEH...
YOUR DIET ISN'T WORTH IT, SIR!

HA! IT IS IF THE DIET HELPS ME SAVE MONEY! AND NOW TO HAVE DONALD INVITE ME TO LUNCH!

WHEN A FELLOW INVITES ANOTHER FELLOW FOR FOOD, COURTESY DICTATES THAT THE INVITOR PAY FOR THE INVITED'S MEAL! I'M NO EXCEPTION—SNEAKY, HUNGRY WOLF THAT I AM!

HERE I AM! WHAT'S COOKIN'?

HORRORS! THAT TABLE IS NAKED! WHERE IS EVERYONE?! DO THEY WANT ME TO WASTE AWAY TO NOTHING?

THE NERVE OF THEM!
BUM BADABOOM

?
POW!

WHY, PRAY TELL, IS IT RAINING YOU?
glxblt
HE WAS ON THE ROOF!
AND THEN HE ROLLED OFF THE ROOF!

FLYING SAUCERS WERE SIGHTED SWIRLING HIGH OVER DUCKBURG...

...SO THE BOYS AND I WERE TRYING TO SNEAK A PEEK! HECK, I'D PAY COLD, HARD CASH TO SEE ONE UP CLOSE!

NUTS TO YOUR LOW-FLYING DISCO PLATTERS! YOU'RE INVITING ME TO LUNCH!
I AM?... GASP LUNCH!

JUMPIN' JUNIPER! I FORGOT ALL ABOUT MY POT ROAST! IT SHOULDA BEEN READY...

...HOURS AGO. WOW. A CHARBROILED CRISPY PAPERWEIGHT.

YEESH! I BURNT MY POTATOES DOWN TO NOTHING...

...AAAAND IT SEEMS MY BROTH IS NOW A BRICK!

HEH... WHO'S UP FOR SOME SANDWICHES?
IS THAT ALL YOU'VE GOT?

DEWEY! PAPER AND PEN, PLEASE!
YES, UNCA SCROOGE!

HMM, LET'S SEE!... GIVEN NORMAL QUALITY FOOD, I'D HAVE EATEN A DOUBLE PORTION OF EVERY-THING! AND AT A GOOD RESTAURANT, I WOULD HAVE SPENT...
LET'S SAY $25, CARRY THE TWO...

...BUT GIVEN YOUR SUBPAR SANDWICHES—APPETITE RUINED—I EXPECT A PROMPT 50% OFF! THAT'S $12.50... PONY IT UP, LAD!
WAK!

EMPTY BELLY, FAT WALLET. NOT BAD!
WAITASEC— WHAT JUST HAPPENED?

HA! DUCKBURG IS SO BUSY SCANNING THE SKY FOR STARSHIPS THAT NOBODY'S GRAZING THE GROUND FOR MISLAID MONEY! COME TO POPPA, HOT STUFF!

YOU KNOW WHAT? IF DONALD INVITED ME TO LUNCH EVERY DAY, I MIGHT ACTUALLY WIND UP A RICH MAN! HA-HA-HA!

WAK!!!

A *THIEF!* TIME FOR A CLOBBERIN'!
WHAT A *PANORAMA!* THIS IS THE BIGGEST COLLECTION OF *FLYWHEELS* I'VE EVER SEEN!

OH! HELLO, FRIEND? YOU A TOURIST, TOO?
NO! I'M A *HOMEBODY!* WHO THE HOOHOO ARE YOU?

O.K.!
NOT HOW YOU *FEEL!* YOUR *NAME! NOMBRE! NOMO! NOMINE! PRÈNOM! NOME! ИМЯ! 名称!*

OH! MY NAME'S *O.K. QUACK...* FROM *PLANET ANATIDAE* IN THE *GOOSEDOWN GALAXY!* MAYBE YOU'VE HEARD OF IT? I'M TOURING THE MILKY WAY IN MY FLYWHEEL!
NOT SEEIN' MUCH *MILK,* THOUGH...
HOW'D YOU GET *IN* HERE?

I UNDID THE LOCK! THAT *IS* HOW DOORS WORK, RIGHT?
TH-THAT'S *IMPOSSIBLE!* I'M THE ONLY DUCK ALIVE WITH THE COMBINATION!

YEAH, BUT I SPEAK A LOCK'S LINGO— CLICKCLICKCLICK! SEE?
YOU ACTUALLY WANT ME TO BELIEVE THAT YOU CAN TALK TO A LOCK?

NO! THAT'S JUST SILLY! WHAT I MEAN IS—LOCKS EXPRESS THEMSELVES WITH MECHANICAL NOISES! THAT'S THEIR LANGUAGE! ANY DUCK COULD LEARN IT... EASY-PEASY-LEMON-SQUEEZY!
SO YOU'RE A DUCKSTRA-TERRESTRIAL? WHERE'S YOUR SAUCER, "D.T.?"

NOT D.T.—O.K.! AND IT'S IN MY POCKET!
HM! DO COPS HAVE RUBBER ROOMS ON STANDBY?

WANNA SEE IT?
HEH! MAYBE A FUNNY FARM!

VOILÀ!
THAT'S ONE OF MY COINS! JUST AS I THOUGHT—YOU ARE A THIEF!

NOT AT ALL! ANATIDAEAN SHIPS SHRIVEL FOR STORAGE! AND THEY EXPAND WHEN THEY READ THE PRINT ON THEIR OWNER'S RIGHT-HAND INDEX FINGER...

VOOMP!

...*LIKE SO!* THAT'S HOW I LEFT ANATIDAE AND FLEW TO EARTH!

WAK! NOW YOU'RE AN *ILLUSIONIST!*

I MAY HAVE LOST MY MARBLES, BUT AT LEAST I CAN MAKE SOME QUICK BANK OFF OF A SILLY SUCKER—I MEAN, LOVING FAMILY MEMBER! HAHAHA!
?

YEAH, UNCLE SCROOGE, I SAID I'D PAY GOOD MONEY TO SEE ONE, BUT—

BUT NOTHING! GET YOUR CASH, BRING THE BOYS, QUIT YOUR JAW-SQUAWKING AND GET HERE NOW!

HOW IS ANY OF THIS NORMAL?
HOW IS ANYTHING WE DO NORMAL? HUSH!

HERE, UNK! $32.50 IS ALL WE'VE GOT! WOULD YOU MIND TELLING US WHY WE RAIDED OUR MONEY RESERVES?
HMPH! $32.50 IS MEASLY...

...BUT I'LL TAKE IT! MINEMINEMINE!
WHATEVER! EXPLAIN ALREADY!

YOU WANTED TO SEE A FLYING SAUCER! WELL, YOU'LL FIND ONE INSIDE MY BIN—WITH THE MATCHING ALIEN AT NO EXTRA CHARGE!
SAY WHAT?

QUACKA-ROONIE!
WAIT... YOU'RE SUPPOSED TO BE AN ALIEN? DRESSED LIKE THAT?!
SAILORS AND CLONES ARE FASHION CHIC?

WELL, IF LOOKS WILL MAKE YA HAPPY...

THIS SPACED-OUT ENOUGH FOR YA?
GAAAH!!!

HOW'S THIS CASUALLY FUZZY MONSTROSITY?
ER... BIGFOOT?

READY FOR MY NATURAL FEATHERY FLUFF, NOW?
SORRY! WE'RE GOOD!

WOW, A REAL-LIFE LITTLE GREEN MAN... LITTLE GREEN-SHIRTED DUCK, ANYWAY... THERE'S SO MANY QUESTIONS I WANNA ASK YOU... BUT I CAN'T THINK OF A SINGLE ONE!
THAT'S NO SURPRISE.

AWRIGHT, NEPHEWS! QUIT GAWKING AT OUR PLANET'S GUEST! AND *YOU*, O.K.— SHRINK YOUR SHIP BEFORE IT CRUSHES MY COINS!

WATCH, BOYS! HE SAYS IT MINIATURIZES BY READING THE PRINT ON HIS RIGHT INDEX FINGER! NEAT, EH?

NOW **GET OUT!** TOO MANY PEOPLE IN MY BIN MAKES ME NERVOUS!
WHAT ABOUT—

ER... YOU DIDN'T COME TO CONQUER OUR PLANET, DID YOU?
NAW! I'M JUST A TOURIST!

ALL I WANNA DO IS SEE THE MILKY WAY AND EXPLORE YOUR PRETTY WORLD!
WELL, KEEP MY VAULT COMBINATION SECRET! I'VE HAD ENOUGH MICRO-DUCKS, FAR-FLUNG ALIENS AND OTHERS AFTER MY CASH!

I COULD ASK YOU... NO, NOT THAT! OOH! MAYBE... NO, THAT'S SILLY—
WE'VE BEEN DOWN THIS ROAD! WE KNOW ENOUGH!

LET'S GO SEE WHAT JUNIOR WOODCHUCK TROOP A IS UP TO! I SAY WE CATCH A BUS—
WITH WHAT FARE? WE GAVE ALL OUR MONEY TO UNCA SCROOGE JUST TO GET A GLIMPSE AT A CURLY-TOP MARTIAN!

CAN WE AT LEAST HAVE MONEY FOR A BUS RIDE, UNCA SCROOGE?
A HANDOUT!? ER, UM... I SEEM TO HAVE SPONTANEOUSLY FORGOTTEN MY VAULT COMBINATION...

I CAN OPEN IT!
KEEP YOUR MITTS AWAY! I REMEMBER!

:GRUMBLE!: EVERYBODY'S ALWAYS AFTER MY MONEY.

$32.50 WASN'T ENOUGH TO FILL A WALLET! SO A DOLLAR A HEAD IS ALL THOSE MOOCHERS GET!

OF COURSE YOU LADS REALIZE THAT THIS IS NOTHING MORE THAN A LOAN—WITH COMPOUND INTEREST!
WE FIGURED AS MUCH!

MR,. McDUCK! I'VE GOT YOUR PAYABLE ACCOUNTS—CHECKED THREE TIMES—AND ALL OF THEM ARE RIGHT!
WHATEVER, CLERKLY! WE'LL SEE AFTER I'VE CHECKED THEM THREE MORE TIMES!

SCRAM! I HAVE WORK TO DO! WHY ARE YOU NUMBSKULLS STILL HERE?
MOSTLY 'CAUSE ANATIDAE ISN'T THIS FUN!

ALSO 'CAUSE MY FLYWHEEL'S STILL IN THERE!
BAH! I'LL GET IT!

IT'S GONE! I PUT IT HERE...
NO ONE CAME IN BUT ME...

UH... WHAT ABOUT THOSE COINS YOU GAVE THE BOYS?
THEY CAME FROM THAT PILE... PLUS... ONE SITTING... ON A BAG
EEP!

CURSE MY KILTS— I GAVE THE BOYS O.K.'S FLYING SAUCER! WE GOTTA CATCH THEM BEFORE THEY CATCH THE BUS!

IT'S ALREADY GONE! WE HAVE TO FOLLOW!

ON FOOT? FORGET IT! HAIL A CAB!
WHO'S PAYING? I AIN'T! AND YOU'RE BOTH BROKE!

GO GET YOUR RATTLETRAP—NOW!
YOU'RE KIDDING! IT'S AT HOME!

QUIT WASTING TIME, WASTREL! GET IT!

...ONE SPEEDING TICKET LATER... GROAN! HOP IN!

SPUTTER... PUTTER... PUTT...
PAP. 271

HUH. YOUR MOTOR'S GOING "SPUTTER PUTTER—PUTT!" THAT "PUTT" IS OFF! YOUR CAR'S SAYING IT'S ABOUT TO BLOW A GASKET!
HE KNOWS THE LANGUAGE OF CAR ENGINES TOO?
313

IMPOSSIBLE! THE ENGINE ON MY TRUSTY 313 WAS RESTORED TWO DAYS AGO AND—
313

WAK! IT WENT OUT IN THE CENTER OF THE INTERSECTION!
GRIND

RUSH HOUR... YET NOTHING MOVES!
BEEP
HONK
HONK
BEEP
HONK
CLANG
BEEP

I OUGHTTA SLUG YOU CREEPS IN THE SNOOT!
YEAH! WE CAN'T *GET* NO PLACE! *ATTAAAACK!*
313

A CRAZY IDEA, BUT TRY *HELP* INSTEAD OF *HARM!* TOGETHER WE CAN ALL *MOVE* THE CAR!

"HELP," YOU SAY?
I S'POSE DAT COULD WORK...
SPLENDID IDEA!

JUST LIFT IT UP... AND CART IT OFF!

YEAH... DIS *TOY LIMOZEEN* DON'T WEIGH NUTHIN'! C'MON! GRAB THE OTHER END!

HEY! GET THAT
EYESORE AWAY!

IT'LL DISTRACT CUSTOMERS FROM MY TEMPTING VEGGIES! TAKE IT TO THE OTHER SIDE!

LET'S DROP IT HERE!
LIKE FUN YOU WILL! I GOTTA LEAVE!

SO WHERE DO WE PUT IT?

ACTUALLY, YOU CAN DROP US OFF AT THE BUS TERMINAL!
WHAT?!

EVERYTHING TO SUGGEST... YET YOU SUGGEST A *TREE.*
AT LEAST IT'S NOT IN THE STREET!

LOOK, PAL—I KNOW *PARALLEL PARKING* IS *HARD,* BUT THIS AIN'T HOW YA PLAY! MOVE IT IN 30 OR I'LL FINE YA!
MY BRAIN *OVERFLOWS* WITH SARCASM.

NOW I GOTTA TRUDGE HOME AND GET MY TOOLBOX! OF ALL THE—
HM? IS THAT—

—IT IS!

QUICK! WHERE'S THE MONEY—
WE ALREADY SPENT IT ON THE BUS RIDE!
BUS STOP

THEN MAYBE THE DRIVER STILL HAS IT...
CALM DOWN! WE'LL PAY YOU BACK! *SHEESH!*

SIR, MY BOYS PAID THEIR BUS FARE WITH *THREE 1942 BRASS DOLLARS,* AND IT'S *IMPERATIVE* THAT WE—
KNOW IF THAT'S THE RATE? YUP!

WELL—ONE OF THOSE COINS WAS ACTUALLY A *FLYING SAUCER,* AND WE THINK YOU'VE STILL GOT IT!
?!?!

IT'S NOT HERE!
NEXT YOU'LL BE TELLING ME THAT THE *BILLS* ARE ALL *SPACE STATIONS* AN' THERE'S A *SPACE WAR* GOIN' ON IN MY BAG!

WHO DID YOU GIVE CHANGE TO?
HOW SHOULD I KNOW? PEOPLE GO IN AN' OUT!
BUS STOP

MAYBE I GAVE CHANGE TO SOME SAP ON HIS WAY TO POLARIS! MAYBE HE PAID HIS TICKET WITH THE MIR SPACE STATION!

MY POOR FLYWHEEL COULD BE ANYWHERE!
THE NUTS YOU FIND ON A BUS ROUTE!
DB31

I CAN'T GO BACK TO ANATIDAE WITHOUT A SHIP! NOW I'M STRANDED ON EARTH!
THIS IS YOUR FAULT! SO HE STAYS WITH YOU UNTIL YOU FIND HIS FLYWHEEL!
ME?!

YES, YOU! YOU'RE THE ONLY DUCK ALIVE WHO COULD FIND IT! EVERY COIN IN CIRCULATION WINDS UP BACK IN YOUR BIN AT SOME POINT!
MY GIFT IS MY CURSE!

NOW EXCUSE ME, BUT I NEED A *TOOLBOX* AND A *TOW TRUCK!*
NICE FELLA.
C'MON, O.K.! *SIGH!* LET'S GO.

BEFORE *ANYTHING,* I NEED TO CHECK THE SUMS OF MY ACCOUNTS PAYABLE!
CLICKETY
CLACKETY
CLINKETA
CLONK

I'LL PUT YOU TO WORK AT *McDUCK INC.,* O.K....
HM...

IT'S *BUSTED.*
LEMME GUESS... YOU SPEAK CALCULATOR SLANG TOO?

ALL MACHINERY! IT *TOLD* ME... A PENCIL STUB WAS WEDGED IN ITS GEARS!
WHAT?...

HANG ON, I'LL RECHECK THE SUMS AGAIN...
CLICK
CLACK
CLICK

MR. McDUCK, I'VE ALREADY EXTRACTED THE *TWO MILLION* WE'LL NEED FOR ACCOUNTS PAYABLE—
NO!!!

OUR SUPER-CALCULATOR WAS *BUSTED!* THE TOTALS ARE *WRONG!* MAYBE FOR *MONTHS!*
WAIT... *WHAT?!*

I *DON'T* OWE TWO MIL, CLERKLY... I ONLY OWE *$1,999,999!*

RETURN THAT EXTRA DOLLAR AT ONCE!

O.K....? WHERE DID YOU GO?

MAYBE I COULD CONSTRUCT A FLYWHEEL OUT OF *EARTH* MATERIALS STURDY ENOUGH TO ZIP ME BACK TO ANATIDAE... BECAUSE YOU EARTHERS ARE *LUNATICS!*

BINK
BONK
BUNK

MAKE ROOM FOR YOUR **NEW GUEST,** *UNCLE SCROOGE! BECAUSE* **O.K. QUACK** *IS STUCK IN DUCKBURG FOR* **QUITE SOME TIME!** *AT LEAST TILL HE FINDS HIS* **COIN** *OR BUILDS A* **NEW SHIP...** *EH, WHICHEVER COMES FIRST!*

THE END...?

Walt Disney's

UNCLE $CROOGE in FRAMING NATURE

WHO'S THAT MISS QUACKFASTER HAS INVITED INTO MY OFFICE? I DON'T LIKE TO START THE DAY WITH SURPRISES!

D 2007-092

Originally published in *Kacer Donald* #12/2011 (Czech Republic, 2011)

AND THEY BRING OUT MY RAW ENERGY AND NATURAL FORCES! OUT!!!

I'LL SPLASH AND DASH OFF SOMETHING MYSELF! WHERE'S THAT PAINT SET I REPOSSESSED FROM DONALD WHEN HE DEFAULTED ON HIS LAST TEN-DOLLAR LOAN?

NATURE? HARUMPF! LIFE? BAH! MY MONEY BIN HAPPENS TO BE MY LIFE!

SOON!
WELL, HERE I AM IN THE MIDDLE OF LIFE, NATURE—AND NOWHERE!

MOO!
THERE'S A DILAPIDATED FARMHOUSE, A SAGGING COW, AND A LOOMING TORNADO... ALL THE REQUIRED RAW ENERGY OF NATURE, REFLECTED IN A SMELLY FROG-INVESTED PUDDLE ON THE RIGHT!
CROAK!

NOW TO CAPTURE IT ALL IN STROKES OF ENERGETIC— OOPS!
CREAK

THIS HILLSIDE IS RIDDLED WITH MOLE HOLES!
BUMP!
BUMP!
BUMP!
CROAK!

I CAN'T GET ANYWHERE WITHOUT THAT CANVAS! GOOD THING A LOCAL YOKEL LEFT HIS RAKE HERE!

A TROGLODYTE WITH FORESIGHT! LUCKY ME!
CROAK!

NOT SO! THERE'S FROG SLIME ALL OVER MY CANVAS!
BUMP

YIKES! A HORNET'S NEST...
WOP

BZZZ ZZZ!
INHABITED BY RAGING HORNETS!

RIP
RAGING HORNETS THAT STING!

FLAP!
OH, FINE! A FROG-REEKING PIECE OF WALL DECORATION WITH VENTILATION!
FLAP!
BZZZZZZZZ

YIKES! THE TORNADO JUST HIT THAT HAYSTACK AND IS HEADING THIS WAY NOW!
MOO!

ROAAR

MY CANVAS! I COULD QUIT RIGHT NOW AND CALL IT "STRAW ENERGY"!
MOO!

BUT AT LEAST THE TORNADO CHASED OFF THOSE HORNETS!
SPLAT!

AFTER ALL THAT GRIEF SALVAGING MY CANVAS, I'M STILL AT SQUARE ONE—PUTTING SOMETHING INSPIRATIONAL ON IT!

I FRANKLY DON'T GET THOSE PAINTERS WHO PAINT FROM NATURE!

IT'S HARD ENOUGH TO PAINT NATURE IN THE FIRST PLACE...

...WITHOUT INTERFERENCE FROM IT!

WHOMP
SPLURT
POP! POP! POP! POP! POP!

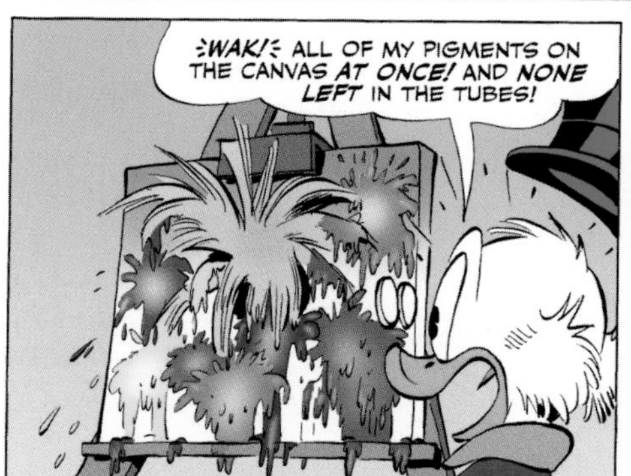
WAK! ALL OF MY PIGMENTS ON THE CANVAS AT ONCE! AND NONE LEFT IN THE TUBES!

PROUD OF YOURSELF, EH, MOLLY?!

SNORT

ER... MOE! I DIDN'T REALIZE YOU WERE A BULL!
SNORT!

BIOLOGY! WHAT WOULD I KNOW?
I'M A PECUNIARY PERSON WHO WANTS...
SLAM!
ZIP!
ZOOM!
...TO GO HOME!

SO... BACK TO THE BIN!
SUCH A WASTE OF EFFORT, PAINT, AND PAIN!

STOP! DON'T!

WHY WOULD ANYONE DESIRE TO DISPOSE OF THIS... THIS... WORK OF STUNNING BEAUTY?!
YOU MEAN...

A UNIT CAPTURING LIFE'S ESSENCE! ITS ENERGY REFLECTING THE DELICIOUSLY ARBITRARY FORCES OF NATURE!
YOU MEAN...

YES! 30,000 DOLLARS!

AND SO...
WH-WHAT'S THE IDEA OF PUTTING ALL THOSE EMPTY FRAMES ON YOUR WALL, MR. McDUCK?

OH, I SEE ONE IS FRAMING A $30,000 CHECK!
AND MORE TO FOLLOW, MISS QUACK-FASTER! MANY MORE!

THEY'LL SHOW THAT CERTAIN SIDE OF ART THAT I REALLY THINK IS WORTH LOOKING AT!
PAT! PAT!
End

Walt Disney's
Uncle Scrooge & Donald Duck

The Great Cackle Caper

BREAKFAST BLOWUPS AT THE DUCK HOME SOUND LIKE THE CALL OF A THOUSAND CACKLING HENS!

WAK! PANCAKES *AGAIN?*

THAT'S ALL WE'VE EATEN FOR *THREE DAYS!*

Originally published in *Almanacco Topolino* #234 (Italy, 1976)

THAT, AND I DON'T HAVE A CHOICE IN THE MATTER! UNCLE SCROOGE FIRED ME FROM MY MONEY BIN JOB... AGAIN.

SLAP
HA!

THEN YOU'D BETTER PRACTICE!

QUIT FRETTING, UNCA DONALD! YOU KNOW UNCA SCROOGE ALWAYS COMES BACK TO YOU IN THE END!

HECK, HE EVEN GAVE YOU A RAISE... ONCE!

YEAH... FROM TEN CENTS TO TWENTY. BIG DEAL!

WELL—ACCORDING TO THIS PAPER, A CALL FROM HIM SHOULD BE COMING SOON!

THE BEAGLE BOYS BROKE OUT OF PRISON! AND UNCA SCROOGE ALWAYS NEEDS YOUR HELP DEALING WITH THEM!

BRRRIIIIIIIINNNNG

HI, UNCA SCROOGE! WE THOUGHT THAT'D BE YOU!

:GRUMPH!: YEAH, UNK?

CHEER UP, NEPHEW! YOUNGSTERS ARE SUPPOSED TO BE CAREFREE AND BRIMMING WITH JOY!

BESIDES, I'VE GOT A NEW JOB FOR YOU! I KNOW YOU'RE... :AHEM: UNEMPLOYED... SO I HAVE A SWANKY LITTLE GIG IN MIND!

I'LL SEE YOU BRIGHT AND EARLY TOMORROW—AND BRING THE BOYS! YOU'LL EACH EARN $2.50 A DAY! WITH ALL FOUR OF YOU, THAT'S TEN WHOLE DOLLARS!

AND SO—THE NEXT MORNING!
I WONDER WHAT'S UP...

TEN BUCKS IS NOTHING TO SNEEZE AT! MAYBE A 24-HOUR BIN WATCH?

YOW! I DOUBT IT! THIS LUNATIC FORTRESS IS GUARDED WELL ENOUGH!

EDWARDIAN CANNONS, LASER GRIDS... ARE THOSE PARTICLE RAYS?! THIS IS IMPRESSIVE!

YEESH! TWO LEVELS OF CLOSED-CIRCUIT TV... UNCA SCROOGE DOESN'T NEED US FOR THIS!

HIYA, UNCLE SCROOGE! WE'RE HERE!
HMF!

NO, NEPHEW! WE ARE NOT "HERE"!
UH... SAY WHAT? HOW'S THAT AGAIN?

BAH! TAKE OFF THAT SILLY HAT!
WHAP

THERE... THAT'S BETTER!

AND THIS HOE WILL MATCH YOUR NEW SUIT!

HOW IS THIS GOOFY GET-UP "BETTER"?
YOU'RE A FARMER!

?
NOW COME ON! TIME'S A-WASTING!

SOON AFTER!
DO YOU CARE TO EXPLAIN THIS, UNK?

ABSOLUTELY! YOU SEE... I'VE DECIDED TO EXPAND MY ECONOMIC EMPIRE!
BY BUYING OKLAHOMA?

NO, BY RAISING CHICKENS! AND PROFITING OFF NOSTALGIA FOR THE OLD DAYS, WHEN FOOD WAS SIMPLE, GENUINE— AND ORGANIC!

AND HOW, PRAY TELL, DO I FACTOR?
YOU "FACTOR" BECAUSE YOU'LL BE MANAGING ONE OF MY RUSTIC FARMS!

YOU'LL BE HANDLING EVERY DUTY! PUBLICIZING THE PLACE ON TV AND RADIO AND DOING INTERVIEWS WITH JOURNALISTS!

N-NOT IF THE DRIVE C-CHURNS JOURNALISTS INTO BUTTER FIRST!
RATTLE
BONK
BUMP

THERE'S A SOLUTION TO EVERY INCONVENIENCE, NEPHEW!

THE FIRST ROUND OF PRESSMEN AND PHOTOGRAPHERS IS ARRIVING BY HELICOPTER!

OLD McDUCK FARMS
No Fowl Play For Our Chickens!
GOOD! THEY'RE HERE!

THIS IS MY NEPHEW, DONALD—LEAD FARMER AND KEEPER OF THE *HENHOUSE!*

YOUR CHICKENS ARE ALL OLD-SCHOOL ORGANICALLY RAISED?
INDEED!

FOLLOW ME AND SEE FOR YOURSELVES!

ADMIRE ALL YOU LIKE! ALSO NOTICE THAT INCUBATOR USE IS BANNED!
AMAZING!

ON TOP OF THAT— OUR ROOSTERS GREET THE SUNRISE WITH *ABSOLUTE* AUTHENTICITY!
COCK-A-DOODLE-DOO!

THAT'S JUST ONE WONDER THIS RUSTIC HOMESTEAD HAS TO OFFER!

OBSERVE! NO HEATERS, AIR CONDITIONERS OR *ANY* NEWFANGLED MODERN CONVENIENCES! EVEN THE *STOVE* IS A BYGONE RELIC!

WE DON'T EVEN USE *WASHTUBS!* JUST AN IRON PITCHER AND A DREAM FOR THE HOMESTEADER!

AND WHO NEEDS A SPRING MATTRESS WHEN *HORSEHAIR* WILL DO?

SMILE, YOU *NINNY!* IMPRESS THEM WITH BOUNDLESS ENTHUSIASM!

WELL, DONALD?
HE'S SO *ENTHUSIASTIC!*
WHAT A *TROUPER* HE IS!

FAREWELL, REPORTERS! *GO!* GO AND MAKE MY FARM FAMOUS!

WELL—I'M OFF! I'VE GOT A BINFUL OF AIR-CONDITIONED MONEY WAITING!
BUT... BUT...

NO BUTS! THERE'S *NO WAY* YOU CAN SCREW UP *THIS* GIG! HAVE FUN, NEPHEW!

DEWEY! HUEY! LOOK! ONE JOURNALIST *DIDN'T* LEAVE!
I'D KNOW A "WIDE-BOTTOM BEAGLE" ANYWHERE!
WE'D BETTER WARN UNCA SCROOGE!

TOO LATE! HE'S TAKEN OFF!

HEY, UNCA DONALD... WE'RE SURE WE SAW A BEAGLE BOY!
THAT'S NUTS! WHAT WOULD THEY BE DOING HERE?

WHAT, INDEED? ANYHOW—FEEDING HENS FOOD AND WATER IS EXHAUSTING WORK! TIME FOR A REFRESHING BATH!

I HAD TO CHOP WOOD, LIGHT A FIRE, AND BOIL MY WATER! REFRESHING... BAH!

AFTER FIFTEEN MINUTES OF BLISS!
UNCA DONALD, SHADOWS ARE LURKING AROUND THE CHICKEN COOP!
WILD ANIMALS, I BET!

ANIMALS WITH BEAGLE SHADOWS?

BEAGLE BOYS STEAL MONEY—NOT EGGS!
OKAY... BUT IF OUR EGGS VANISH, THAT'S STILL A PROBLEM!

THERE'S A RUSTED SHOTGUN IN THE DEN!
FILL IT WITH ROCK SALT AND SPOOK WHATEVER'S OUT THERE AWAY!

AND SO...
WHO NEEDS REST? THE THINGS I ENDURE FOR $2.50!

HERE GOES NOTHIN'... OPEN THE DOOR!
QUIT WORRYING! NOW YOU'RE MAKING ME NERVOUS!

IF ANYONE'S IN HERE... DON'T MOVE!

WAK!

BETRAYAL!
THUNK
THUNK

BANG

GET BACK TO YOUR NESTS! IT'S JUST ME!
IS SOMETHING... SHIMMERING?

HEY! HOW COME THIS EGG'S SO SHINY?
I BET I CAN VENTURE A GUESS...

GOLD! 18-KARAT HEN FRUIT!
18K

THAT'S THE KIND OF EGGS THESE CACKLING MONSTERS SPECIALIZE IN?!
PLOP

GASP! SO THAT'S UNCLE SCROOGE'S GAME...

NOW IT MAKES SENSE! WHEN UNCLE SCROOGE LEARNED THE BEAGLE BOYS BROKE OUT OF JAIL, THIS FARM NONSENSE BECAME HIS STRATEGY!

THAT MONEY-NUT HAD HIS GOLD INGOTS MELTED DOWN INTO GOLD EGGS! HE'S HIDING THEM HERE TILL HE CAN MOVE THEM SAFELY!

WHO'D EVER THINK OF LOOKING FOR GOLD IN A CHICKEN COOP?
WHAT AN UNCLE!
176-716

"RUSTIC FARM," MY EYE! WE BEAGLES KNEW EXACTLY WHAT THIS WAS!
AND NOW WE PLAY THE PLANNING GAME! HEEHEE!

UH-OH... THAT MEANS THERE WERE BEAGLES MIXED INTO THAT PRESS CONFERENCE!
WHICH ALSO MEANS THEY'LL BE PLANNING A THEFT— SOON!

THEN WE'D BETTER FIND THE OTHER GOLDEN EGGS AND RE-HIDE THEM IN A SAFER PLACE!

BUT...
OW! THAT HURT!
NO ONE COULD GET EGGS FROM THESE ATTACK BUZZARDS!

THUS...
A FORCED RETREAT! HOW SHAMEFUL!
UNCA SCROOGE KNEW WHAT HE WAS DOING, HIDING HIS GOLD HERE!

MAYBE THAT'S GOOD! SO ALL WE HAVE TO DO IS ADD EXTRA SUPPORT FOR "BEAGLE RESISTANCE!"
WHAT'S OUR PLAN, THEN?

HM! WE'LL GUARD THE COOP IN TWO-HOUR SHIFTS!

DEWEY, YOU'LL GO FIRST! THEN HUEY, THEN LOUIE! I'LL GO LAST!

THUS THE GUARD PLEASANTLY SHIFTS UNTIL, AT LAST... DONALD...
ALERT AND AWARE! YAWN!

BUT THINGS GET TOO "PLEASANT" AS OUR GUARD NODS OFF...
HERE WE GO, BROS! HIT THE GROUND AND DON'T MAKE A PEEP!
ZZZ!

THIS LAUGHING GAS IS JUST TH' THING FOR TURNIN' MEAN CHICKENS CHICKEN!
HA! AND TURNIN' DUMB DUCKS' FROWNS UPSIDE DOWN!

SPEAKING OF DUMB DUCKS... DONALD'S ON WATCH! SO THIS'LL BE A CINCH!

MASKS ON, MEN! PUMP THAT GAS AND MAKE 'EM LAUGH!

BOK! BOK! BOK! BOK-HAW-HAW!

WHUH? I'M SO SLEEPY I FEEL... GIDDY?

UH-OH! HAHAHA!

CHEERFUL COMPANY, ISN'T IT?
QUIT THE GABBIN' AND GET TO WORK, 176-761!

HM! TH' GOLD ISN'T VISIBLE ON THE OUTSIDE, I GUESS!
CLUCK-HAW-HAW!

VERY SOON!
GOT 'EM ALL!
LET'S BOUNCE, BROS!

GULP! NOISES IN THE COOP!
I HOPE NOTHING SERIOUS HAS HAPPENED TO UNCA DONALD!

ALL THE EGGS ARE GONE!
NOT TO HIM! JUST TO HIS INTEGRITY!
GONE... THE EGGS, MY INTEGRITY, AND MY GOOD-WILL WITH UNCLE SCROOGE!

THOSE SCAVENGING SNEAKS USED GAS TO KNOCK ME OUT OF COMBAT!

BUT LET'S SEE THEM OUTRUN US ON THIS AWFUL—

...RO-O-OAD!
BUMP!
CLUNKITY!
CLANK!

UH-OH! FOUR PESTIFEROUS WARTS OFF THE PORT BOW! TIME TO GAS IT, BROS!

WHAT KINDA KOOKY GREASED LIGHTNING WAS THAT?
ZOOM
ZOOM

I'M BROKEN! I'M BROKEN!
SKRANG

WHY DIDN'T YOU *STOP* WHEN YOU HEARD OUR SIREN?!
THAT'S WHY!

...INJURED MY INNOCENT CAR... AMBUSHED ME IN A CHICKEN COOP... AND ALL FOR WHAT? FAKE GOLDEN EGGS!

FINALLY! YOU'RE BACK! GET ME DOWN OFF THIS BLASTED ROOF!

THAT CRAZED CHANTICLEER CORNERED ME! RUN HIM OFF!
I'VE HALF A MIND TO LEAVE YOU STRANDED!

SIGH! HAVE AN EGG, CAMILLA! YOUR GONZO SERVICES ARE NO LONGER NEEDED!
BOINK

WHERE ARE MY OTHER EGGS? DO YOU EVEN CARE ABOUT MY FARM? WHAT'S WITH YOU?

WHAT'S WITH ME?! I JUST RISKED MY SKIN DEFENDING YOUR GOLDEN EGGS FROM THOSE STINKING BEAGLES!

GOLD EGGS? NEPHEW, ARE YOU NUTTY IN THE NOODLE?

DON'T YOU "NUTTY NOODLE" ME! LOOK! GET OUTTA THE WAY, YOU!

DON'T TELL ME YOU DIDN'T KNOW ABOUT THAT!
DONALD... I DIDN'T!

GOLD EGGS... REAL GOLD EGGS!

YOU SWEET THING! YOU BEAUTIFUL CACKLING CREATURE!
BOK-BOK!

YOU DESERVE AN EXTRAORDINARY RATION OF FEED FOR THIS! BUT FIRST...

CAN YOU MAKE ME ANOTHER? PRETTY PLEASE? FOR OL' "UNKY SKOOGE"?

ONE EGG A DAY ISN'T ENOUGH! I'VE GOT TO FIND THE FORMULA FOR HOW THESE CHICKENS—
HELLO, SCROOGE!

YOU! WHAT DO YOU WANT? YOU SOLD ME THIS FARM! I'VE RENAMED IT—

WELL, OF COURSE, SUH! BUT I'M HERE FOR MY GOLD EGG! I DIDN'T SELL YOU THAT!

THAT'S RIGHT, GIRL! GIVE THAT PRIZE BACK TO OL' COLONEL KENTUCKY!
BOK-BOK!

YOU CAN BARGAIN FOR IT IF YOU LIKE, SUH! BUT FOR NOW, YOU'LL JUST HAVE TO DO WITH THE GRADE-A NATURALS!
PRETTY SURE HE WANTS THE WHOLE HOG!

THIS EGG AND I GO WAY BACK! AS YOU CAN SEE, IT WAS MY PRIZE AT THE COUNTY COMPETITION!
1ST PLACE
FOR BEST CHICKEN
WEBFOOT COUNTY FAIR

ALL THIS OVER A FAKE! AAARGH! WHAT'S WORSE—YOU OR THOSE BLASTED BEAGLES?! NOW I'VE LOST THOUSANDS IN EGG SALES, AND YOU'RE GONNA REPAY EVERY LAST CENT!
I SUPPOSE THAT'S BETTER THAN GETTING FIRED.

YOU KNOW WHAT?... YOU'RE RIGHT. AND YOU'VE ALSO GIVEN ME AN IDEA! YOUR NEW JOB IS SECURE!
UH... OKAY! WHAT'S THE WORK?

YOU'LL FIND OUT ONCE YOU ARRIVE AT MY MONEY BIN TOMORROW!
UH...

THE FOLLOWING AFTERNOON!
SO WHAT DO YOU SUPPOSE UNCA DONALD'S NEW JOB IS?

GUARDING THE BIN, I GUESS!
ALL THE OTHER PROTECTION HAS DISAPPEARED!

SWANKY, UNCA DONALD!
YEAH! YOU'RE THE SOLE GUARD FOR THE WHOLE WORKS!
ER... YEAH, BUT THERE'S A REASON...

QUACKAROONIE! THE BIN IS EMPTY!
WHERE'S THE MONEY?
UNCLE SCROOGE DISGUISED IT AND SENT IT AWAY!

DON'T TELL US HE TURNED IT INTO EGGS!
NO... INSTEAD IT'S... UH, SOMETHING LIKE BUTTER? HE HID IT IN A DAIRY NEAR THE HARBOR... BUT HE DIDN'T TELL ME WHERE!

NOPE. BYE, UNCA DONALD!
YOU MAKE A GREAT GUARD...
...WHEN THERE'S NOTHING TO GUARD AT ALL!
SIGH!
END!

WALT DISNEY'S GYRO GEARLOOSE

THE TERRIBLE THINKING CAP TUSSLE

AS GYRO TESTS HIS LATEST INVENTION—SOARING SLACKS WITH BELL-BOTTOMED BOOSTERS—SINISTER EYES IN TRIPLICATE ARE WATCHING...

SMOOTH AS AN AIRBORNE BABY'S BOTTOM!

MERP!

S 4143

Originally published in *Anders And & Co.* #46/1965 (Denmark, 1965)

BUT THE BEAGLES SOON LEARN THAT IT ISN'T SO EASY TO FLY BY THE SEAT OF ONE'S PANTS! MUCH LESS CRAM A 40-INCH WAIST INTO A 32-LONG...
HEY! WHADDAYA THINK YOU ARE... A FANCY-PANTS?
YI-I-I! IT'S HARD TO BALANCE IN THESE BRITCHES!
176-123

THEN LAND, STUPID!
OKAY!
176-123

AND "LAND STUPID" IS EXACTLY WHAT HE DOES!
YEEEOW! THESE BRITCHES SURE AIN'T COBBLESTONE-PROOF!

I'VE GOTTA GET UP AND COOL OFF MY... ER... LANDING GEAR!
176-123

HEY-HEY! WATCH WHERE YOU'RE GOING!
176-123
176-231

AWK! HE DENTED THAT ARMORED CAR DOME FIRST!
McDUCK
YOU FEEL SOMETHING, CHAUNCEY?
JUST A FACE-FIRST BEAGLE BARRAGE, EDGAR!

-AWK!- STUN ROUNDS! TIME TO TAKE 176-321 IN TOW!
THOSE AWFUL BEAGLE BOYS ARE ALWAYS TRYING NEW NASTY METHODS TO ROB US!
McDUCK BUCK TRUCK
176-123
176-321
PEW! PEW!

BACK TO GYRO! A SOFTHEARTED RUBBISH COLLECTOR HAS GIVEN HIM A RIDE HOME...
WELL! IT SURE BEATS WALKING, ANYHOW!

THANKS MUCH, FRIEND!

AND A LITTLE LATER...
-GRRR!- THOSE FLYING BRITCHES WERE NEARLY THE END OF US!
-HMM!- I THINK I KNOW WHAT THE TROUBLE WAS!
LAB DRAB LAB

YOU WERE JUST TOO BIG FOR MY BRITCHES! HA-HA-HA!
-GRRR-GRRR-GRRRR!-

NOW WE'LL JUST HELP OURSELVES TO ALL OF YOUR GOOD INVENTIONS!
B-BUT THEY'RE ALL GOOD!
PIPE DOWN!

DIG THIS NUCLEAR SLINGSHOT!
176-123
CHECK OUT THIS MUSCLE-MILK!
176-321
AN' THIS "CARPET RUNNER"!

SHH!
THINKING CAP
OW! YOU DUMB RUG!

HUH! A WEIRD KIND OF HAT FELL ONTO MY HEAD!

WHAT'S THAT TOPPER DOIN' TO YOU, 176-123?
OH-OH! HE'S WEARING MY THINKING CAP!
HMM! HMM! HMM!
MAN! LISTEN TO THE HMM-ING BIRDS!
176-123

WOW! WHAT A BRAINSTORM THIS BIRDIE-BONNET GAVE ME!

I NOW KNOW HOW TO ROB THE SECOND NATIONAL BANK OF DUCKBURG... IN MY SPARE TIME... WITHOUT GETTING CAUGHT!
176-123

FELLAS, THIS THINKING CAP IS WORTH MORE TO US THAN TEN TONS OF NORMAL INVENTIONS!
I VOTE WE TAKE IT!
ME, TOO! THE AYES HAVE IT!

NO NO, FELLAS... WITHOUT MY THINKING CAP I'LL BE NOTHING BUT A... A BIRDBRAIN!
TOUGH STUFF! HAR-HAR-HAR!

WELL, I'D BETTER REPORT THE THEFT RIGHT AWAY!

POLICE! THE BEAGLE BOYS STOLE MY THINKING CAP FOR SINISTER PURPOSES!
THEN THAT EXPLAINS IT!...

THE SECOND NATIONAL BANK OF DUCKBURG HAS JUST NOTIFIED US THAT ALL THEIR MONEY IS GONE, AND THEY CAN'T IMAGINE WHO DID IT, OR HOW!
GONE... EVERY RED CENT!
AND EVERY GREEN BUCK!
BUT I'VE BEEN AT THE DOOR ALL THE TIME!

THERE'S JUST A FEW ANTS LEAVING NOW!

BUT A CLOSER LOOK AT THE SO-CALLED "ANTS"...
WE'RE SO SMALL NO ONE NOTICES US!
HO HO! IMAGINE, THE TOWN'S BIGGEST ROBBERY BEING PULLED BY SUCH SMALL FRIES!

AND THE MONEY IS SMALL, *TOO...* IN THESE BAGS!
ALL WE HAD TO DO WAS TURN THE SAME *REDUCING-RAYS* ON THE MONEY THAT WE USED ON OURSELVES!

AT THIS RATE WE CAN CLEAN OUT THE *WHOLE TOWN* IN RAPID ORDER!

...AND WE'LL STORE ALL OUR LOOT IN *HERE!*
YEAH! *HA-HA!* THIS *TINY* SHACK WILL HOLD *MILLIONS 'N' MILLIONS* OF DOLLARS... WHO WOULD *GUESS* IT?

AND SO IT GOES...
CRIME WAVE! READ ALL ABOUT IT!
ER—NO THANKS, SONNY... IT'LL MAKE ME ILL!

DUCKBURG GOING BANKRUPT!
IT'S DRIVING ME CUCKOO... KNOWING MY THINKING CAP IS BEHIND IT ALL!

AND *WITHOUT* THE CAP'S SUPPLEMENTARY STIMULATION, I CAN'T IMAGINE HOW THE ROBBERIES ARE DONE!

GYRO, IT'S UP TO *YOU* TO DO SOMETHING NOBLE AND SAVE THE CITY!
ER... YOU'RE RIGHT, CHIEF O'BULL!

I GUESS I'LL HAVE TO BUILD *ANOTHER* THINKING CAP!
GOOD GRIEF! IS *THAT* ALL YOU HAVE TO DO?

WELL, IT'S NOT QUITE AS SIMPLE AS IT SOUNDS...

...AFTER CONSTRUCTING THE ROOSTING PLACE WITH ITS NETWORK OF BRAIN-IMPULSE RELAY CIRCUITS...

...I HAVE TO CATCH SOME HMM-ING BIRDS!

...AND THE ONLY PLACE THE BIRDS INHABIT IS THE "HMM-ING" PLANET OF LITTLE THINKLE-STAR!

NOBODY'S LOOKING...

...SO I'M OFF TO LITTLE THINKLE-STAR IN MY ROCKET-POWERED WATER TOWER!
WHEN TOWERS FLY, I START WALKIN'!

MERE HOURS LATER, GYRO ALIGHTS ON LITTLE THINKLE-STAR...
YAY! THERE ARE LOTS OF HMM-ING BIRD NESTS STILL AROUND!

OH-OH! BUT THEY'RE ALL EMPTY!

-GULP!- IT LOOKS LIKE THE HMM-ING BIRDS HAVE BECOME *EXTINCT!*
WHAT A TRICK FOR THEM TO PLAY ON ME!

THEN, JUST AS GYRO IS ABOUT TO GO HOME EMPTY-HATTED...
-EH?- MY *ANTENNA* IS ACTIVATED!
HMM!
BOING!

WHY, THEY'RE *NOT EXTINCT!* THEY JUST *MOVED UP* IN THE WORLD!

YAY! THREE OF THEM!

OOPS! SPIRITED BIRDS, TOO! THERE GOES ALL MY AIR!
KA-POW!

HMM-ING BIRDS COMING THROUGH! *FEET AND LUNGS,* DON'T FAIL ME NOW!

NOW TO CONTEND WITH THE BAD BEAGLE BOYS ON EARTH!

AND IN NO TIME AT ALL, GYRO'S NEW THINKING CAP IS DOING BRILLIANT WORK!
WOW! NOW I REALIZE WHAT THE BEAGLES ARE DOING AND HOW TO COUNTERACT IT!

I MERELY HAVE TO BUILD A REDUCING-RAY REVERSER...
WORKSHOP

...AND THEN TURN IT ON ALL OF DUCKBURG UNTIL I FIND THE BEAGLE BOYS!

TCH-TCH! THOSE BAD BOYS MUST HAVE EVERY CENT IN TOWN! EVEN BILLIONAIRES ARE BEGGING!

I'VE COVERED DOWNTOWN! NOW I'LL WIDEN MY CIRCLE TO INCLUDE THE SUBURBS...

EH? SOMETHING'S POPPING BELOW!

EEK! WE—AND ALL OUR LOOT—SUDDENLY BECAME FULL-SIZE AGAIN!
THAT SHACK LITERALLY EXPLODED WITH WEALTH!

NOW TO LAND AND CAPTURE THE CULPRITS!

I'M TOO MUCH OF A BRAIN NOW TO BRAIN YOU FOR THIS! LET'S SETTLE IT... BRAINWAVES TO BRAINWAVES!
WAVE-ON!

HMMMM! HMMMM! HMMMM!
HMMMM! HMMMM! HMMMM!

UNGH! THIS LOOKS LIKE A THREE-BIRD TIE! EH? ACTION'S STIRRING UPSTAIRS!

HMM!
HMM!
HMM!
HMM!
POP!
GREAT SHIFTING BALANCES!... AND BABY MAKES FOUR!

YAY! HALF-A-HMM MORE WAS ALL WE NEEDED!
CUCKOO!

DUCKBURG IS SAVED FROM RUIN, AND I NOW HAVE THE MAKINGS OF A SUPER THINKING CAP!

ONLY THIS TIME I'LL TAKE SECURITY MEASURES... HMM!
HMM!
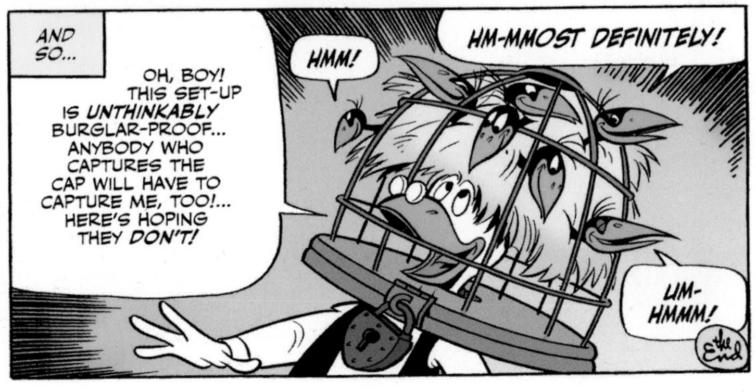
AND SO...
OH, BOY! THIS SET-UP IS UNTHINKABLY BURGLAR-PROOF... ANYBODY WHO CAPTURES THE CAP WILL HAVE TO CAPTURE ME, TOO!... HERE'S HOPING THEY DON'T!
HMM!
HM-MMOST DEFINITELY!
UM-HMMM!
the End

Walt Disney's Uncle $crooge in Waste Makes Haste

Originally published in *Kalle Anka & Co.* #47/2014 (Sweden, 2014)

DID YOU SAY... GOLDEN?
¦SIGH!¦ UNFORTUNATELY, HE DID!

NOT SO FAST, HUCKSTER! IS THIS ANOTHER SUREFIRE, CAN'T-MISS SCHEME OF YOURS?
AW, SHUCKS! YOU GUESSED!

IT BETTER BE GOOD! I PAID FOR FLOOR-CLEANING FIVE YEARS AGO!
GOOD? WHY, IT'S THE MARVEL OF A MILLENNIUM!
FIRST, WE PLACE THE SECRET CONTENTS OF THIS BOX INTO AN ORRR-DINARY WASTEBASKET!

THEN WE TAKE THIS CONTRACT DRAFT THAT YOU WERE GOING TO DISPOSE OF... ONE I'M SURE SNOOPY COMPETITORS WOULD LOVE TO READ...

...SO, LET'S MAKE SURE THEY NEVER DO, EH?

MOST FIRMS USE COSTLY PAPER SHREDDERS TO DESTROY DOCUMENTS! BUT DIRECT YOUR WIDE EYES BASKETWARD!

FLOOOF!
!

AMAZING!
MY NEW LOW-TECH ALTERNATIVE TO SHREDDERS!

IT'S JUBAL POMP'S MINI-MITES! PAT. PENDING! TERMITES TENDERLY TRAINED BY YOURS TRULY TO EXCLUSIVELY SEEK THE SMELL OF PAPER! IT TOOK A WHOLE YEAR TO TRAIN THEM!

THEY ONLY CHEW PAPER—AND THEY'RE FAST! ONE MINI-MITE CAN GO THROUGH A WHOLE SHEET IN SECONDS!
DID YOU JUST SAY...

...TERMITES?!?
YES! THAT'S WHY I NEED YOUR INVESTMENT CAPITAL, PARTNER! YOU SEE, I STILL MUST—

ARE YOU OUT OF YOUR BUG-BREEDING MIND? BRINGING PAPER-EATING PREDATORS TO A BIN FULL OF BANKNOTES?
NOT PAPER-EATING... PAPER-CHEWING! LIKE SCISSORS! AND THEY DON'T—

GREAT GADFREY!
SLIIIP!

CA-RASSH!
THE TERMITES! THEY'RE LOOSE! MY PAPER CURRENCY IS DOOMED!

FEAR NOT, MY FRETTING FRIEND! I TRAINED THE 'MITES ONLY TO LIKE THE SCENT OF ORDINARY PAPER! SEE? THEY BALK AT BUCKS!
WHEW! THAT'S A RELIEF!

EEEEEK!

CALAMITY, MR. McDUCK! BUSINESS CONTRACTS ARE BEING VORACIOUSLY VOIDED!
THOSE TERMITES ARE TOO FAST! STOP THEM, POMP!

ER, UM, AND HOMINA... I CAN'T! I NEEDED YOUR INVESTMENT FOR RESEARCH ON, ER... TRAINING THEM TO STOP!

I'M PHONING A BUG EXPERT!
BELAY THAT! TOO COSTLY! THIS AMATEUR ENTOMOLOGIST AND I WILL ROUND UP THE SWARM OURSELVES!

SCREEECH!

THAT SCREAM CAME FROM MY ACCOUNTING DEPARTMENT!
MOTHER O' PEARL! THOSE 'MITES DO MOVE!

EEEEP!
OPPP!
ORRRK!
AAAAAH-AH!
HAH! GOT 'EM!
LEMME HAVE A LOOK!
SORRY, OL' SOCK! YOU DIDN'T CATCH "THEM"... YOU ONLY CAUGHT ONE MINI-MITE!
ONE?! JUST ONE INSECT CAUSED ALL THIS CHAOS?
WELL, THEY ARE THE VERY MODEL OF A MODERN MAJOR BREAKTHROUGH! BUT THE OTHER MITES—
ENOUGH! BACK TO THAT EXPERT!
TO THINK I LET YOU BURST IN HERE WITH ANOTHER CRACKBRAINED SCHEME!
IF IT'S ANY CONSOLATION, YOU HAVE MADE THAT MISTAKE BEFORE!
NO LOANS!

SOON! THE EXPERT VISITS...
I'VE CONDUCTED EXTENSIVE TESTS ON THIS MINI-MITE, AND DISCOVERED A SMELL IT LIKES EVEN MORE THAN THAT OF PAPER!
SET UP A FEW ANT TRAPS WITH THIS SMELL, AND YOU'LL HAVE THOSE TERMITES CAUGHT IN NO TIME!
ER... WHAT SMELL?
G'WAN! GIT!

McDUCK LIMBURGER EXTRACT!

AND I JUST SPRAYED MY MONEY WITH—
URK!

AND LEFT MY VAULT DOOR OPEN! NOW I KNOW WHERE THE...
...OTHER MITES ARE!

LISTEN, OLD TOP! I HAVE A MUCH BETTER IDEA FOR HOW WE COULD—
HUSH! AND KEEP TAPING THOSE BILLS TOGETHER!
the End

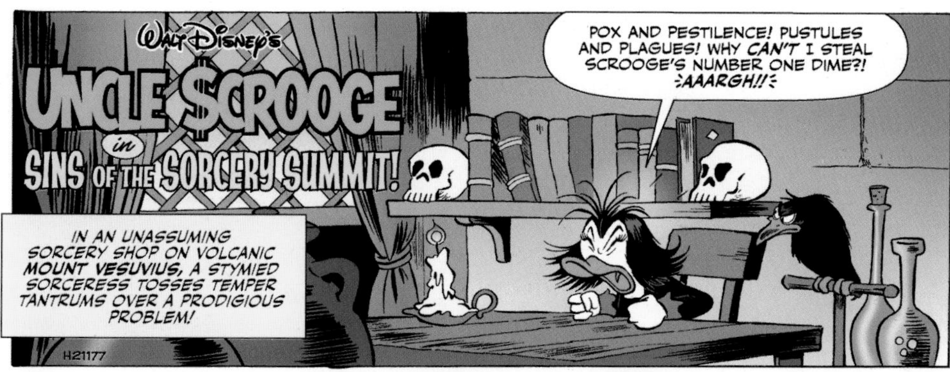

Originally published in *Donald Duck* #44/2014 (Netherlands, 2014)

RATFACE DOES HIS DUTY WELL!
MESSAGE FOR YOU, MIM!
MAGNIFICENT! MARVELOUS!

CATCH, WITCH HAZEL!
YEA VERILY, BLACK RAVEN!

NOW TO FIND WITCH WINIFRED! LAST I HEARD OF HER, THAT KOOK WAS FIGHTING OVER CHRISTMAS TREES—

HM! BUT FIRST, A PITSTOP AT THE McDUCK MONEY BIN!

FEH! A BORING OLD MISER AND HIS BORING OLD BUSINESS!

AT LEAST HE'S LEAVING! NOW I CAN SNOOP UNDISTURBED!

HOLD MY CALLS, EMILY! I'M OUT FOR LUNCH!
NOT WITHOUT YOUR HAT, YOU'RE NOT!

OOPS! I'D FORGET MY HEAD IF IT WASN'T STUCK TO MY NECK!
HANG ON! I'LL GO GRAB YOUR TOPPER, MR. McDUCK!

?
HEY!

SCRAM, YOU FILTHY SQUAWKING BUZZARD!
SKRAWK!

WHAT WAS THAT?
A RAVEN! PROBABLY ATTRACTED BY THE SUN SHINING ON YOUR COINS!

THE NERVE! CLOSE THAT WINDOW, MISS QUACKFASTER!

IF EVERY BEAST AFTER A SHINY COIN GOT IN, I'D BE POOR IN 10,000 YEARS!
?

THANKFULLY, MY NUMBER ONE DIME IS ALWAYS UNDER GLASS!
UH... MR. McDUCK! THAT RAVEN WAS HOLDING A LETTER!

WAK!
BAD NEWS, SIR?

ABSOLUTELY AWFUL! MAGICA DE SPELL IS RECRUITING A GANG OF WITCHES TO STEAL MY DIME! I HAVE TO HIDE IT! BUT WHERE?!

ONE WEEK LATER, NEAR DUCKBURG HARBOR...
HEY, MISTER! WHAT ARE THOSE RUINS OUT THERE?
HUH? OH... THAT'S OLD FORT LOCKMAN!

INTERESTING! IS IT OPEN TO THE PUBLIC?
I GUESS YOU COULD RENT A BOAT! BUT WHY? ONLY NUTS GO THERE!

REALLY NOW? WHY IS THAT?
THAT JOINT IS SPOOKED! THE ISLE'S A DOLLED-UP HAUNTED HOUSE!

IT'S KNOWN FOR FREAKY WEIRDNESS! THE LAST FEW NIGHTS IT HAS ECHOED WITH THE VOICE OF A GHOSTLY SOLDIER!
SHOUTING AS HE MARCHES... LEFT! RIGHT! LEFT! RIGHT!

ABOUT FACE! C'MON, PHIL! WE'RE GOING TO THE BEACH!
WHATEVER YOU SAY!

ARE THE WEIRD STORIES ABOUT FORT LOCKMAN TRUE, UNCA DONALD?
ALL STORIES HAVE MERIT. BUT I'D HAVE TO SPEND A NIGHT THERE AND JUDGE FOR MYSELF.

DO YOU WANNA?
UH, WELL...
OF COURSE HE DOESN'T!

YOUR UNCLE CAN HARDLY MANAGE A NONHAUNTED HOUSE!
GLADSTONE! EITHER BLOW AWAY...

...OR SAY IT TO MY FACE, YOU WASTE OF SPACE!
OH, MY! LOOK AT ALL THE CRABBY DUCKS!

DO YOU WANNA VISIT FORT LOCKMAN OVERNIGHT, COUSIN GLADSTONE?
DO I LOOK LIKE A CRAZED THRILLSEEKER?

HA! SO THE LUCKY BOY FINALLY ADMITS HE'S JANGLED!
WATCH YOUR TONE! FINE... I DARE!

LET'S MAKE A DEAL! $100 TO THE DUCK WHO STAYS LONGEST!
PREPARE TO PAY, LOSER!

PERFECT! NOW WE'LL DECIDE WHICH OF YOU GOES FIRST!
WHAT? WE'RE NOT GOING AT THE SAME TIME?

HECK NO! THAT'S WAY TOO EASY A DEAL!
WE'LL TOSS TO SEE WHO STAYS THE FIRST NIGHT! HEADS—UNCA DONALD! TAILS—COUSIN GLADSTONE!

WELL?
IT'S—

MEANWHILE—LET'S SEE HOW MAGICA AND RATFACE FARE!
SKRAWK! I'M BACK, BOSS LADY!
WELL? HOW DID IT GO?

EH. NO WORRIES.
PERFECT!

AND DID YOU GET A LOOK AT THE NUMBER ONE DIME?
OOPS!
ER...

N-NO! SCROOGE WAS... THERE! WANDERING HIS OFFICE... MENACINGLY! YEAH... THAT'S NOT A LIE AT ALL!
EH-HEH...

NO MATTER! TOGETHER, MY WITCHY WOMEN AND I WILL KNOCK HIS SPATS OFF!

THEN I'LL MELT HIS DIME AND CAST AN AMULET—GIVING ME THE MIDAS TOUCH AND MAKING ME ALL-POWERFUL!

ARE YOU GONNA SHARE THAT POWER WITH THE WITCHES?
DO I LOOK THAT INSANE?

GRAAAAH! THAT POWER AND WEALTH WILL BE MINE!
YUP. INSANE.

THAT EVENING!
YOU WON'T STAY TO CALM MY NERVES?
NOPE! WE ABSOLUTELY REFUSE!

WE LEFT YOU A BOAT IN CASE FORT LOCKMAN BECOMES UNBEARABLE!
IT'S ON YOU TO ACCOMPLISH YOUR BRAGGA-DOCIOUS FEAT— OR FLEE!

GOOD LUCK, UNCA DONALD!
THANKS LOADS. SIGH!

CALM DOWN, DUCK! YOU KNOW GOOD AND WELL THAT GHOST SOLDIERS DON'T EXIST!

LEFT! RIGHT! LEFT, RIGHT! UP! DOWN! LEFT! RIGHT!
!!!

WHAT'S THE CONSENSUS, MEN? IS UNCA DONALD FULL OF BALONEY?
WELL, TO BE HONEST—

SEE YOU AT HOME, BOYS!!!
SPLISH
SPLASH
SPLOSH

WELL, THAT'S WORRISOME. HE LASTED LONGER THAN I EXPECTED, THOUGH...
FORT LOCKMAN AND UNCA DONALD... WHAT A POWERFUL MESS.
WOW.

NEXT DAY!
I KNEW YOUR UNCLE WAS SCARED OF HIS OWN SHADOW! HA-HA-HA!

I GUESS OUR DEAL'S DONE! I'LL GET MY $100 AND I DIDN'T EVEN HAVE TO... SNIFF ...WORK TO EARN IT!
NOTHIN' DOIN', BRAGGART!

UNCA DONALD STAYED AT FORT LOCKMAN TEN MINUTES! EITHER YOU LAST LONGER, OR YOU FORFEIT!
BRRR! FINE...

UPSTAGING DON IS A HASSLE... BUT IN THE END, ONLY MY HAPPINESS MATTERS!
YEAH, WE'LL SEE!

ELSEWHERE, THAT NIGHT— THE SORCERY SUMMIT BEGINS!
PRITHEE, WHERE BE WITCH WINIFRED?
THE KOOK'S PROBABLY STUCK IN A TREE! LET'S GET ON WITH IT!

THE THREE OF US CAN EASILY BOLLIX THAT RICH, WHISKERY QUACK!
YES, BUT HOW?

WITCHERY!
HONEY, THAT'S A GIVEN! NOW WOULD HE BETTER AS A TOAD, OR A—
WAIT! I HEAR NOISES!

?
LADIES, I THINK FATE JUST PLAYED RIGHT INTO OUR HANDS...

NIGHT PASSES AND MORNING BREAKS... WITHOUT COUSIN GLADSTONE!
WHERE ON EARTH IS HE?
HE'S PROBABLY TOO LAZY TO ROW HIS BOAT!

IT'S ALMOST TEN A.M.! SHOULD WE WORRY?
WITH HIS LUCK, HE'S TOTALLY SAFE... RIGHT?

HE'S BEING SELFISH! HE WANTS YOU TO GO PICK HIM UP!
WELL, WE'RE GOING TO LOOK ANYWAY!

AND SO...
GLADSTONE'S BOAT... IT'S GONE!
THAT'S WEIRD! IT'S ALSO IMPOSS-IBLE!

IF HE'D MADE IT BACK TO THE PIER, WE DEFINITELY WOULD'VE SEEN HIM!
GLADSTONE! COUSIN GLAD-STONE!

WELL?
NOTHING!
NOT EVEN A STRAY RABBIT'S FOOT!

LOOK! IN THOSE BUSHES! GLADSTONE'S HAT!

OKAY, NOW I'M WORRIED! CAN LUCK SAVE A GUY FROM A GOSHAWFUL DROP?

AND WHILE THE DUCKS FRANTICALLY SEARCH FOR GLADSTONE— SCROOGE GETS THREE UNEXPECTED VISITORS!
IN AN *INVULNERABLE FLYING BOAT!*
SMASH!!!

THAT'S WHAT MY GANG'S *INNATE MAGIC* CAN DO! NOW HAND OVER THAT DIME!
NEVER!

THEN TELL ME WHERE YOU HID IT, YOU CREAKY COOT!
HIT THE BRICKS! YOU'LL NEVER FIND IT!

SO YOU WANT TO PLAY, EH? SEE THAT ISLAND? "HAUNTED" FORT LOCKMAN!

THAT'S WHERE WE HELD OUR SORCERY SUMMIT! NOW, BE A DARLING AND GUESS THE *GUEST* THAT I'VE TRAPPED THERE?
SANTA CLAUS?

NOPE! YOUR NEPHEW—GLADSTONE GANDER!
BIG DEAL!

YOU *BET* IT'S A BIG DEAL! BECAUSE IF YOU DON'T GET THAT DIME, MY "LADIES' COTILLION" HERE WILL UNLEASH A *SUPER SPELL!* AND YOU'LL NEVER SEE YOUR NEPHEW AGAIN!

I DON'T BELIEVE YOU! PROVE IT!
PROVE WE SHALL, THOU ODIOUS DUCK!

THAT'S A BARREL OF MY EXPLOSIVE HEX DUST, BUSTER! IT'LL TRANSFORM FORT LOCKMAN INTO A GIANT WEST HIGHLAND WHITE TERRIER... AND GLADSTONE INTO A FLEA!

YOU LOONIES WOULD MUTATE AN ENTIRE ISLAND FOR ONE MEASLY LITTLE DIME?
COUNT ON IT!

WHAT IF I GIVE YOU MY NUMBER TWO PENNY INSTEAD? OR A NUMBER THREE NICKEL?
BAH!

I'M SURE I'VE GOT A 1988 UGLY QUARTER STASHED AWAY—
MIM! HAZEL! GRAB HIM!

LET'S SEE YOUR BIG BEAK MAKE EXCUSES WHEN YOU'RE STUCK TO A BARREL OF HEX DUST, McDUCK!

LEMME GO!
NOT BEFORE YOU GIVE ME THAT DIME! LET'S JET, LADIES!

HELP! I'M TRAPPED IN A HORRIBLE WAKING NIGHTMARE!
ZOOOOM

SOON ENOUGH!
HALP!
SCROOGE, YOU AND YOUR KIN ARE BOTH GETTING A DOSE OF REAL BLACK MAGIC!

GASP! WHAT THE DING-DONG BLAZES?

THY BIRD HATH FLOWN!
"THY BIRD" AIN'T CALLED A LUCKY GANDER FOR NOTHIN'!

MY PATIENCE IS NIL! TIE HIM UP AND LIGHT THE FUSE!

EITHER YOU TELL ME WHERE THAT DIME IS IN TEN MINUTES, OR—BOOM—YOU TURN FLEA, AND WE PUT ON THE DOG!

C'MON, LADIES! WE NEED TO FIND SCROOGE'S NEPHEW!
WHAT FOR, MAGICA?

BECAUSE GLADSTONE IS GOING TO HELP US KILL TWO BIRDS WITH ONE STONE... HEH!
HOW SO?

WE USE YOU GIRLS' MAGIC TO SUCK AWAY HIS LUCK! THEN WE FIND THE DIME, EASY!
MAGNIFICENT!

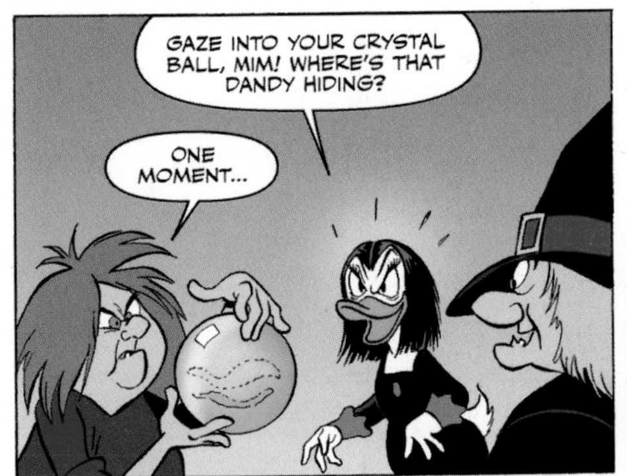
GAZE INTO YOUR CRYSTAL BALL, MIM! WHERE'S THAT DANDY HIDING?
ONE MOMENT...

BLISTERING PUS-POCKETS! THIS ISLAND IS FILTHY WITH DUCKS!

YE THREE KIDS ARE HARMLESS! BUT WE'LL TEACH YON ROGUE DONALD!
WHERE ARE THEY?

SHUSH! TALK SOFTLY, DEARIES! THEY'RE UP ON OUR ROOF AND COMING DOWN!
ODS BODKINS! THAT MEANS—

MEANWHILE! THE MINUTES LEFT FOR UNCLE SCROOGE TO SAVE HIMSELF ARE TICKING AWAY!
GREAT HONK! IF I DON'T REVEAL MY DIME'S HIDING SPOT, I'LL BE HIT WITH THE WORLD'S WEIRDEST WHAMMY!
FSSSSST...

WHAT AN AWFUL CHOICE! GIVE AWAY OLD NUMBER ONE... OR GET INSECTIFIED BY A GANG OF LADY MOUSTACHE-TWIRLERS!
FSSSST...

I'LL NEVER AGAIN SWIM IN MY MONEY! OR DIVE IN IT LIKE A PORPOISE! OR TOSS IT UP AND LET IT HIT ME ON THE HEAD!
FSSSST...

ALL RIGHT, MAGICA... YOU WIN! THE DIME IS—
STOP TALKING!
FSSST...

FSSSSST...
BOYS? BOYS!
ALWAYS HERE AND RIGHT ON TIME!

WHAT ON EARTH HAPPENED?
WE FOUND GLADSTONE AND FREED HIM FROM THIS DUNGEON!

BUT MAGICA AND THE WITCHES—
HA! WE SORT OF SNUCK UP ON THEM!

SEE... WE'D BROUGHT A JUNIOR WOODCHUCK ANTI-SPOOK BLOCKER, JUST IN CASE!
A FISHNET SOAKED IN GARLIC JUICE, TO CLOAK OURSELVES AND KEEP MAGIC OUT! EXCEPT—

HAH! IT ALSO KEEPS MAGIC IN!
ONE OF THESE DAYS, McDUCK! ONE OF THESE DAYS!
MAKE ROOM, MIM! THOU ART HEFTY!

WE'D BETTER GO GET THE COPS... OR AN EXORCIST!
HANG ON, LADS!

I'M NOT LEAVING WITHOUT MY NUMBER ONE DIME!
IT'S HERE?!

WHERE DID YOU HIDE IT?
I'LL GLADLY SHOW YOU!

SEE—THIS ALL STARTED WHEN I LEARNED MAGICA'S MOB WAS COMING TO TOWN! I THOUGHT... NOWADAYS, BARELY ANYONE VISITS FORT LOCKMAN! AND THAT MADE IT THE PERFECT DIME-HIDING PLACE!
TILL MAGICA CAME HERE TOO!

AH, BUT EVEN SHE NEVER GUESSED!
I'VE VISITED THE DIME'S SECRET LOCATION EVERY NIGHT!

FROM HERE... LEFT, RIGHT, LEFT, RIGHT, UP, DOWN, LEFT, RIGHT!
LEFT, RIGHT, LEFT, RI— OH NO...

YOU'RE THE "GHOST SOLDIER" I HEARD! I LOST $100 OVER A DIME!
SOME HERO! AFRAID OF HIS OWN UNCLE! HAHAHA!

THAT'S WHY I WON THE MONEY AND YOU'LL ALWAYS BE A LOSER! PAY UP!
WHAT?!

YOU DARE TO HIT ME UP FOR CASH AFTER I SAVE YOUR LIFE!
A DEAL'S A DEAL, DUCK!

QUICK, PHIL! GIMME THAT PAPER! WEIRD SOLDIER NOISES FROM FORT LOCKMAN!
WHAT IS IT? MORE OF THAT "LEFT, RIGHT, LEFT, RIGHT"?
NAW! COMBAT PRACTICE! WHAMS, BAMS, AND BODYSLAMS! LOTS MORE FUN TO LISTEN TO!
End

Originally published in *Topolino* #2183 (Italy, 1997)

Walt Disney's

MAGICA DE SPELL in BELLE, BOOK AND BUNGLE

Originally published in *Anders And & Co.* #9/2014 (Denmark, 2014)

AND FUN IS GIVING "HOT LIPS," HERE, THE BOOT!

KA-ZOW!

KA-POOF!
KA-SLAM!

KA-OUCH?!

SO, WHAT'S BEHIND THE SIX-RING CIRCUS, SCROOGE?
HARUMPH! I RECEIVED A PARCEL WITH A DRAGON STATUE, SUPPOSEDLY FROM ONE OF MY ITALIAN BUSINESS CONTACTS!
WHEN I UNWRAPPED IT, THE DRAGON CAME TO LIFE... AND TRIED TO MAKE OFF WITH MY NUMBER ONE DIME!

HAD I NOTICED THE POSTMARK WAS MOUNT VESUVIUS, I'D HAVE SMELLED DE SPELL—MAGICA DE SPELL, THAT IS!
WHO? NEVER HEARD OF HER! WELL, AT LEAST I SAVED YOUR DIME!

SHOULDN'T THAT MEAN A REWARD?
WHAT?! IS YOUR HAND OUT FOR A HANDOUT?

IN A WORD, YES! WHY, JUST THIS MORNIN', MY PAL CAPTAIN ANNIE SAID...

YARR! I HATE TO MENTION IT, BELLE, BUT YER BOAT NEEDS REPAIRS—BAD!
AND AS USUAL, I'M BROKE!
S.S. GILDED LILY

SO, SINCE YOU AN' I ARE GOOD FRIENDS—
DO YOU THINK I'M MADE OF MONEY?! ...DON'T ANSWER THAT! MY OWN REPAIRS WILL RUN INTO THE HUNDREDS!

HMPH! IT SEEMS TO ME THAT BELLE DID STOP THE THEFT OF YOUR FAVORITE KEEPSAKE!

GRUMBLE! I SUPPOSE YOU ARE ENTITLED TO SOME SORT OF FINDER'S FEE FOR SAVING THE DIME!

AND—SINCE A FINDER'S FEE IS USUALLY 10% OF THE FOUND OBJECT'S VALUE, HERE'S A NICE SHINY PENNY FOR YOU!

NOW THAT YOU'VE BEEN DULY COMPENSATED, I HAVE A BUSINESS TO RUN!
SCROOGE McDUCK ...is not in!
SLAM!

ONE CENT? JUST WHEN YA THINK HE CAN'T SET THE STINGINESS BAR ANY LOWER!
KINNEY'S KAFÉ

HOWDY, EVERYONE! NICE DAY, ISN'T IT?
GRROWL! NOT IF YOU'VE GOT A THROBBING GOOSE-EGG ON YOUR HEAD, AND A BADLY BATTERED BACKBONE! OUCH! OOCH!

THIS PENNY IS ALL I COULD SQUEEZE OUT OF THAT MERCILESS MISER SCROOGE McDUCK! Y'ALL GOT ANYTHING FOR ONE CENT?
YOU JUST INHALED IT, LADY!

ER... DID YOU JUST WALK INTO McDUCK'S OFFICE? LIKE, WITHOUT ANYONE STOPPING YOU?
I SURE DID, KID! SCROOGE AND I GO WAAAY BACK!

MAGICA, OLD GIRL, YOU MAY BARELY BE ABLE TO MOVE—BUT YOU'VE JUST STUMBLED ONTO THE PERFECT WAY OF GETTING SCROOGE'S DIME... WITHOUT MOVING! OUCH!

YOU SOUND A BIT LOW ON FUNDS! CARE TO DO SOME ODD JOBS FOR ME WHILE I REST AND GET HEALTHY?
IF THERE'S CASH IN IT, I'M THERE, SUGAR!

SPLENDID! YOU SHOULD KNOW I... UM, DABBLE A BIT IN... ER, MAGIC—AS A HARMLESS HOBBY, OF COURSE. I COULD USE YOWCH! AN ASSISTANT!

AND, ONCE MY BLACK MAGIC HAS CORRUPTED THE FOOL, I'LL MAKE HER WALK STRAIGHT INTO McDUCK'S OFFICE...
...AND SWIPE THE NUMBER ONE DIME OOOCH! FOR ME!
RAT'S NEST HOTEL

MY HOTEL ROOM! I USUALLY STAY HERE WHEN I'M IN TOWN ON ※UGH!※ *BUSINESS!*
HOO-WEE! TAKE IT FROM ME, KID! WHATEVER BUSINESS YOU'RE IN... *GET OUT!*

NEVER MIND THAT! I NEED TO *REST* MY ※OOORG!※ *BACK!*
THERE'S AN *UNFINISHED GHASTLY GHOUL-LASH* THAT NEEDS MIXING! MY BOOK OF FEARSOME FORMULAS AND RANCID RECIPES SHOULD—

BA-BOOMF!

WHAT GIVES?

GREAT CIRCE! WHAT HAVE YOU *DONE?!*
I LIT TH' BUNSEN BURNER, THREW SOME HERBS INTO THE POT, AN'... *BA-BOOMF!*

WHAT IN THE WORLD COULD HAVE GONE *WRONG?* THAT RECIPE HAS *NEVER* FAILED BEFORE!

GET SOME *WATER,* SO WE CAN WASH AWAY THESE BLOBS OF *ANTI-GRAVITY GOO!*
AYE-AYE, CAP'N!

ONE BLOB-WASHING LATER!
DONE! OUCH!
WHILE YOU WERE BUSY, I STARTED SOME POTS SIMMERIN' AN' USED THIS STICK TO STIR 'EM—WEARIN' GARDEN GLOVES FOR SAFETY, O' COURSE!

THOSE GLOVES ARE VERY VALUABLE! THEY PROTECT THE WEARER FROM THE EFFECTS OF ALL MAGIC!
YOU DON'T SAY?

SO... MAYBE MY STIR-FEST TURNED THIS STICK INTO A MAGIC WAND! CATCH!
NO, DON'T—

PLUFF!

STOP! ...ARRGH, MY BACK!
I DECLARE! MOVES LIKE SCROOGE THAT TIME WE WENT BARN-BOOGYING! WONDER HOW IT REACTS TO MUSIC!

WHAT NOW? INVOLUNTARY DANCING?

GIVE ME THAT, YOU JINX!

AND BACK TO A SEDENTARY STATE FOR YOU!
UN-PLUFF!

NOW—I'D LIKE TO KNOW EXACTLY WHERE YOU FOUND ALL THOSE BIZARRE CONCOCTIONS!
OH, I NEVER EVEN LOOKED AT THAT BOOK! I DON'T FOLLOW RECIPES!

YOU DON'T?
HON, WHAT'S THE POINT OF MAGIC—OR COOKING—IF Y'ALL CAN'T HAVE A LITTLE FUN WITH IT? IN FACT, I... I, AAH... I, AAH-AAAH...

...CHOOOO!

MY BOOK! IT... IT TURNED INTO SOLID STONE!
NO MORE LIGHT READING, EH? SO THAT'S WHAT MY MAGIC POWDER DOES!

SPUTTER! MAGICA DE SPELL DOESN'T NEED AN IMBECILE AS A SORCERESS' APPRENTICE! YOU'RE FIRED! AND WITHOUT PAY!
MAGICA DE SPELL? YOU'RE MAGICA DE SPELL?!

TAKE OFF THOSE GLOVES AND GET OUT, YOU STAIN ON SORCEROUS SAFETY!
WELL! IF YOU SAAAY SO...!

I DO SAY...
...UM, SAY... SAY, MY BACK IS CURED!

THE DANCING MUST HAVE FIXED IT! AND NOW I'M GETTING A DEVILISH IDEA!
TOODLES, KIDDO!

A WAVE OF THE WAND, A HOOT ON THE HORN, AND THEN... THE UNTHINKABLE! CHORTLE!
MELODIOUS MONK'S Music
MOVING SALE

SAY, SPORT... I ONLY HAVE ONE CENT, BUT I REALLY NEED TWO PAIRS O' THOSE!

ANOTHER GREAT GROUP DISCOUNT LUNCH AT BERTRAM BURGER! SORRY IT WAS YOUR TURN TO GO BURGERLESS, FRED—

GREAT GLOBS OF GRAVY! MY MONEY BIN... GONE!

DON'T YOU WORRY, HON! I'LL HELP YOU FIND IT... ONCE YOU'VE PUT ON THESE EARMUFFS!

EARMUFFS? WHAT IN THIS WAKKED-OUT WORLD DO THEY HAVE TO DO WITH MY BIN?
OH... WITH A LITTLE LUCK, THEY'LL PROTECT US AGAINST THAT!

WAK!
LOOKS TO ME LIKE SHE'S LEADIN' THE DANCING BIN INTO THE DEEPEST PART OF THE TULEBUG RIVER!

SHE'LL JUST SWIM INTO MY OFFICE FOR THE DIME—AFTER BREAKING THAT PRICEY PICTURE WINDOW SHE DIDN'T MELT EARLIER!
I JUST CAN'T WIN!

YES, YOU CAN, SUGAR! THERE'S A WAY WE CAN STOP HER IN TIME! COME...

AHEAD, PERIL LOOMS LARGE!
HELP! EEK! SCREECH!
WE'RE DANCING STRAIGHT TOWARD THE RIVER!

I HATE TO END THE BALLET, MAGICA...

...BUT YOU FORGOT SOME-THING!
THE ANTI-GRAVITY GOO!

YOU WON'T STOP ME, ONCE YOU SINK LIKE A ROCK—COURTESY OF...

...MY NEW STONE BOMBS!
KA-VOOF!

COUGH! COUGH!
COUGH!

TH-THE BOMB! IT DIDN'T WORK?
NOPE! I GOT WORRIED MAGICA WAS UP TO SOMETHING, SO I TURNED HER ANTI-MAGIC GLOVES INSIDE OUT...
...SO ONLY SHE'D GET HEXED BY THE STONE POWDER! EVERYONE ELSE WOULD BE PROTECTED!

SEEMS TO ME LIKE I ONCE AGAIN DESERVE A FINDER'S FEE! SO... WHAT'S TEN PERCENT OF THREE CUBIC ACRES O' CASH? HMMM?
!

ULP! LET'S SKIP ALL THAT BORING MATH! WHY DON'T I JUST FOOT A FULL REFURBISHING OF YOUR RIVERBOAT INSTEAD... EH?... HUH?
HOW SWEET! I ACCEPT!

CHEER UP! YOU GOT A NICE NEW GARGOYLE TO PUT BY YOUR PURTY PICTURE WINDOW!
the End

Walt Disney

Glittering Goldie's Grandkid

DICKIE DUCK

CELEBRITY CRUSHED

Dear Journal,
When it comes to helping friends in need, **how** can I say no?

YOU'RE *FINALLY* HERE, DICKIE!

CAME AS FAST AS I COULD SHAKE IT! HOW'S THE... *SITUATION,* DAISY?

Originally published in *Topolino* #3045 (Italy, 2014)

"...And the undying fandom that came with!"
WHAT'S UP? YOU GIRLS TRYING TO FLOOD THE HOUSE?
WHO CARES? WE'VE BEEN DUMPED! SNIFF!

SAY, NOW! WHO ARE THESE BEAUTY BOYS?
THE QUACKER BOYZ! IT'S FOR THEM WE PINE, BUT TODAY ON FACEBEAK...
BOYZ

...THEY ANNOUNCED THEIR JOINT ENGAGEMENT TO THE GIRLS IN DUCKSTINY'S CHILD! HOW COULD THEY?!
WAK!
SWISH
The drama thickened!

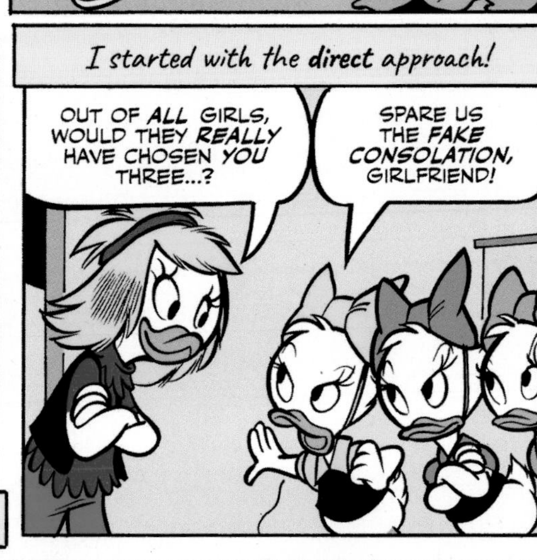
I started with the direct approach!
OUT OF ALL GIRLS, WOULD THEY REALLY HAVE CHOSEN YOU THREE...?
SPARE US THE FAKE CONSOLATION, GIRLFRIEND!

That didn't work! Maybe a little logic...
AW, THOSE QUACKER BOYZ ARE PART OF A CRAZY HOLLYWOOD FANTASY WORLD! AREN'T THERE ANY GUYS AT SCHOOL...?
PHOOEY!

THEY'RE ALL FREAKS, GEEKS, AND MAMA'S BOYS! THEY'LL NEVER MATCH JIM, TIM, AND ERIC!
Houston, we had a problem!

I kept trying to burst that bubble...
MEH... ON SECOND THOUGHT, THEY'RE NOT SO HOT! I'VE SEEN CUTER!
SAY WHAT?!
ARE YOU BLIND?! THOSE EYES... THAT HAIR... THOSE BEAKS...
TRUST ME! IN TEN YEARS, THE WORLD WILL BE FULL OF GLAMOUR GUYS BEATING DOWN YOUR DOOR!
This was it! Time to get real...
...with the honest-to-goodness truth!
FAME AND STYLE AREN'T EVERYTHING! YOU'VE GOTTA ACTUALLY KNOW A CRUSH TO LEARN HIS TRUE QUALITIES!
Exquisite, Dickie! Ten points!
GOSH, DICKIE, MAYBE YOU'RE RIGHT!
THIS MIGHT JUST BE A PASSING CHILDISH FANCY!
CORRECTAMUNDO! EVEN I HAD A CRUSH ONCE! YOU'LL GET OVER IT!
BUT WHAT'LL WE DO TILL THEN? WE'RE JUST HEARTBROKEN!
Easy! Find a delicious distraction!
LET'S FORGET OUR TROUBLES WITH A BIG CONE OF GOOSEBERRY ICE CREAM!
YAY!!!

I figured the simplest, most **caloric** solutions worked best!
SLURP! *TRIPLE-BERRY!* NOM!
HEY, WHAT'S BUZZIN' OVER THERE?

SOMETHING'S GOING ON OVER AT THE WALDORK HOTEL! WOW!
THE WALDORK

HURRY, JENNY! IT'S *JOHN CUQUACK!* WE'VE *GOTTA* GET HIS AUTOGRAPH!
THERE HE IS! ***EEEEE!!!***

J-JOHN CUQUACK? *MY* EX-CRUSH HOLLYWOOD HEARTTHROB!

Dear Journal, who was **I** to squash three kids' **undying fandom?**
YOO-HOO! HEY, JOHNNY! I LOVE YOU!
After all, I **am** still a kid, too... right?
END

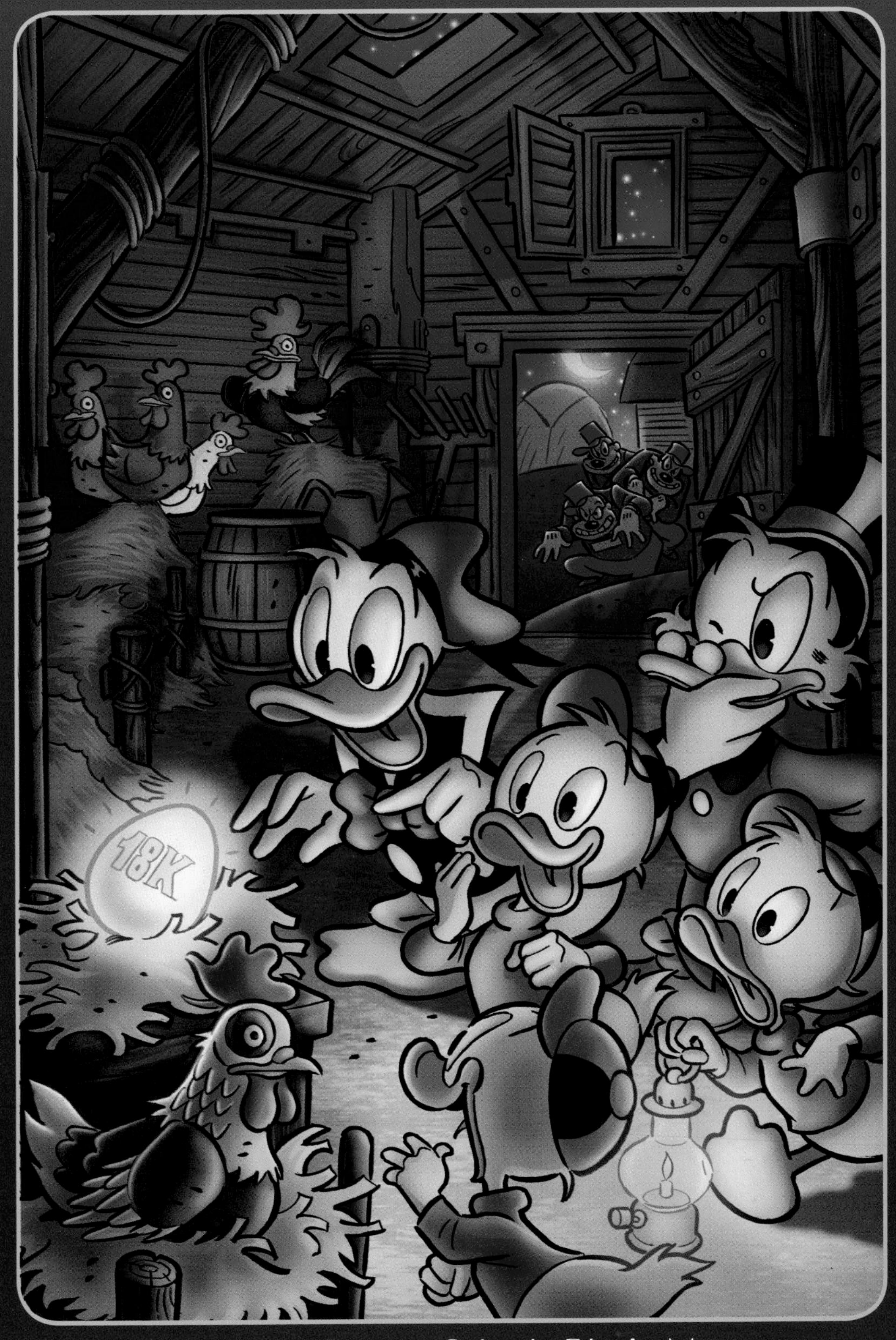

Art by Andrea Freccero, Colors by Fabio Lo Monaco

Art by Corrado Mastantuono

Art by Massimo Fecchi, Colors by Mario Perotta

Art by Giorgio Cavazzano, Colors by Max Monteduro and David Gerstein

Art by Alessio Coppola, Colors by Max Monteduro

Art by Marco Mazzarello, Colors by Mario Perotta

Art by Daan Jippes and Ulrich Schroeder, Colors by Sanoma

Art by Corrado Mastantuono, Colors by Corrado Mastantuono & Ronda Pattison

Art by Marco Gervasio, Colors by Marco Colletti

MORE FUN-FILLED ADVENTURES
ARRIVE IN A BRAND-NEW COLLECTION!

ON SALE NOW

WRITTEN BY
JOEY CAVALIERI
& JOE CARAMAGNA
ART BY VARIOUS

"IF YOU ARE A FAN OF CLASSIC DISNEY AND *DONALD DUCK* COMICS, OR *DUCKTALES* (THE OLD AND THE NEW), THIS COMIC WILL BE A GREAT READ FOR FANS OF EVERY AGE."
—*COMICOSITY.COM*

FULL COLOR · 72 PAGES
$9.99 US / $12.99 CA
ISBN: 978-1-68405-230-1

WWW.IDWPUBLISHING.COM